HOW KOALA
Lost his Tail

and other Australian stories

HOW KOALA
Lost his Tail

and other Australian stories

by L&G Adams

COLLINS

Sydney • London

Volume I

First published 1984 by William Collins Pty Ltd, Sydney
Reprinted 1987
Printed by Dai Nippon (Hong Kong) Ltd
National Library of Australia
Cataloguing-in-Publication data
Adams, L. (Lee)
How koala lost his tail and other Australian stories.

ISBN 0 00 101249 5.
[1]. Aborigines, Australian – Legends – Juvenile
literature. I. Adams, G. II. Title.
398.2'049915

CONTENTS

HOW KOALA
Lost his Tail

There was a time, long ago, when the land was struck by a terrible drought. Everything was parched and dry as far as the eye could see.

Each day the animals looked at the sky, hoping for clouds to bring some precious rain.

But the rain clouds never came. The rivers and lakes soon dried up. The ponds and waterholes became empty and the animals grew thirstier and thirstier with every passing day.

This was a time when Koala still had a tail. It was long and bushy and he was very proud of it.

One hot, thirsty morning Koala was sitting under a shady tree. He had just begun fanning his face with his tail to make a cool breeze when Kangaroo came over and sat beside him.

"I remember a drought when I was young," Kangaroo said. "If my mother had not found some water, we might have died."

Koala pricked up his ears.

"Your mother found water?" he asked. "My dear Kangaroo, where did she find it?"

"She searched everywhere until she found a dried-up river bed," said Kangaroo. "She dug a deep hole and a little water seeped into the bottom of it. There wasn't much, but it saved our lives."

Koala jumped up.

"Could you find that river bed again?" he asked excitedly.

"I suppose so," Kangaroo answered.

"Then come on," Koala urged as he tugged at Kangaroo's paw. "If we can find the river bed, we can dig a deep hole and get some water. I'll help with all the digging. I promise!"

So Koala and Kangaroo went off to find the river bed.

For some time they searched through the trees. As the sun rose higher, the day became hotter and hotter and soon Koala began to pant and moan.

"My dear Kangaroo. I can't walk any further," he sighed. "Would you be a good fellow and carry me?"

"Carry you?" Kangaroo asked, surprised.

"Certainly," replied Koala. "If I were a bigger, stronger creature, I would gladly carry you. Friends should always help each other."

"Very well," agreed Kangaroo. "Climb on my back."

"Thank you, my dear friend," said Koala happily as he scrambled up. "Off you go now."

With Koala perched comfortably on his back, Kangaroo trudged on and on in the terrible heat.

As the day became hotter, Koala seemed to grow heavier and heavier. Kangaroo carried him for hours, but could finally go no further.

Just as he was about to give up, he came out of the trees. He suddenly stopped, hardly able to believe his eyes. There, right in front of him, was a familiar place.

"This is it!" Kangaroo shouted. "This is the river bed!"

"Well done, my good fellow," said Koala as he climbed down from Kangaroo's back. "I knew we could find it."

"You start digging the hole," Kangaroo panted. "I need a rest."

"No, you start digging," Koala called out as he hurried into the trees. "I'll go and find us something to eat. We need it after that tiring walk."

Before Kangaroo could say anything, Koala had disappeared.

Kangaroo walked wearily to the middle of the river bed and began to dig. The ground had been baked by the sun and was as hard as rock. Soon Kangaroo's paws were cracked and bleeding.

Koala did not really go looking for something to eat. He simply sat under a tree and had a sleep. When he woke a little later, he returned to the river bed.

He walked over to the hole Kangaroo was busily digging and peered inside.

"That isn't very deep yet," Koala said. "Never mind. We'll soon find water."

Kangaroo popped his head out of the hole.

"It's your turn to dig," he said. "And where's my food?"

"My dear friend. I couldn't find any," Koala answered. "I searched everywhere. I'm so tired now, I need a little rest."

"But ... " began Kangaroo.

"Tut tut," Koala interrupted. "There's no need to thank me. After all, that's what friends are for."

Koala lay in the shade of a nearby bush while Kangaroo began digging again.

The hole in the river bed slowly grew deeper. Poor Kangaroo's claws were broken and sore and he ached all over.

"I can't go on," he thought. "Koala will have to dig now."

He walked towards Koala but Koala saw him coming. He quickly shut his eyes and began to twitch and mumble to himself.

"Water, water," he moaned.

"Poor little thing," Kangaroo thought as he looked down at Koala's twitching body. "He's so worn out that he's talking in his sleep. I suppose he does need a rest. I'll wake him later."

Kangaroo went back to the hole. The sun blazed down and his throat was as dry as dust.

"I must keep digging," he thought. "I must find some water."

He scratched and scraped until at last he knew he could dig no more. But just as he was about to give up, the earth at the bottom of the hole became damp. A tiny trickle of water appeared.

"Water!" Kangaroo shouted. "It's water!"

He jumped up excitedly.

"Koala, here it is!" Kangaroo shouted. "Water!"

Before Kangaroo could say another word, Koala rushed to the hole.

"My dear, wonderful fellow," he squeaked happily as he pushed Kangaroo aside. "I knew we could do it. Make way now!"

Koala hopped into the hole and greedily drank the water.

"It's delicious," his voice echoed up from the hole. "Really delicious! But I'm sorry to say there's hardly enough for two."

This made Kangaroo rather annoyed.

"That selfish Koala," he muttered. "He hasn't helped me one little bit. And now he's taking all of the water for himself!"

Most of Koala was hidden in the hole. Only his long, bushy tail was visible, waving in the air.

Kangaroo listened as Koala lapped up the last few precious drops of water.

"I'll teach him a lesson," he thought angrily.

Kangaroo bent down. With one swift snap of his teeth, he bit Koala's tail right off!

Koala gave a horrible shriek and raced into the bush.

"That'll teach you to be so greedy!" Kangaroo called after him.

"Yiii!" Koala cried. And that was the last Kangaroo ever saw of him.

All this happened a long time ago. But you'll be pleased to know that the drought soon ended. The rain clouds arrived and the rivers and ponds filled with water once again.

Today koalas are much nicer creatures. They are quiet and helpful, and they would never dream of being greedy or mean.

For their missing tails still remind them of that koala of long ago, and how his selfishness made them lose their tails forever.

HOW ECHIDNA
Got his Quills

In the very beginning the world was empty and silent. There were no animals in the bush. No birds to sing their songs. No pretty butterflies to flutter along. Even the trees stood quietly, for there was no gentle breeze to whisper through their leaves.

When the Great One saw that the world was empty, he made creatures to fill it. As he created each one, he gave it something to keep it from harm.

To Dingo he gave strong teeth. To Eagle he gave swift wings. To Native Cat he gave sharp claws. To Crocodile he gave great jaws. To Owl he gave eyes that could see in the night. To Kangaroo he gave long legs to run swiftly in flight.

But when at last he came to Echidna, the Great One had nothing left to give. Nothing at all.

With nothing to keep himself safe, Echidna knew that soon the other animals would try to eat him. So he quietly crept away. But as he was crawling into a bush, he overheard the other animals talking.

"I'm feeling hungry," said Dingo, snapping his teeth.

"I want to eat," growled Native Cat, stretching her claws.

"There's no sense in hunting each other," hissed Python, flicking his tongue in and out. "We're all too strong. But I know someone who can't fight or bite."

"What?" said Dingo in surprise. "Can't fight or bite? Who can it be?"

"Echidna," answered Python.

"Anyone who can't fight or bite must have been made to be eaten," purred Native Cat. "Let's eat Echidna."

"Yes, let's eat Echidna," said the others hungrily.

Poor little Echidna shivered with fright. "I must find the Great One," he thought. "I must ask him to find me some long legs or sharp teeth or wings that can fly. I must find him, or I shall die."

Not daring to make a sound, Echidna quickly hurried off.

All through the hot, dry desert Echidna searched. But he wasn't really sure what the Great One looked like. So it was very hard to find him.

"I don't suppose the Great One lives here at all," said Echidna, resting his weary paws. "The sun is much too hot."

He looked towards the distant horizon and saw a long, green line that marked the end of the desert and the beginning of the bush.

"Perhaps he lives over there, where everything is nice and green," he thought.

Just as Echidna was setting off, a cloud of dust came swirling and whirling across the desert. Closer and closer it came until it turned into a fearsome shape. It was Dingo following Echidna's trail!

Off to the distant bush Echidna shuffled as fast as his little legs could run. "What a lovely meal I'm going to have," growled Dingo as he drew closer. But just as he pounced, Echidna reached the edge of the scrub and dived into a big clump of thorny bushes.

"I must find the Great One," whimpered Echidna, emerging from the bushes. He had left Dingo sniffing around on the other side.

All through the bush Echidna searched. He peeked under the rocks and peered high into the trees. He crept into dark caves and crawled through the thickets. But the Great One was nowhere to be found.

"I know," said Echidna as he spied something in the distance. "He must live by that billabong. Everything there looks nice and cool."

Just as he waddled off, he heard a rustling noise above him in the trees. Down sprang Native Cat, scratching and screeching and laughing with glee.

Poor little Echidna would have been eaten on the spot if Dingo hadn't suddenly arrived. Dingo had been so busy following Echidna's trail, he bumped right into Native Cat.

Native Cat got quite a shock. Dingo jumped back in surprise.

"He's mine!" screeched Native Cat.

"He's mine!" growled Dingo.

And with both his enemies close behind, poor little Echidna raced away.

Through the bush he ran, with Native Cat and Dingo snapping hungrily at his short, stumpy tail. Soon he came to the tall, thick reeds that grew beside the billabong.

"Oh dear. How will I get across to the other side?" he cried. "If only the Great One had given me some swift wings or long legs."

Echidna cried so loudly, he woke up Python who had been sleeping in the reeds.

"What's this?" hissed Python, rising over the reeds to see better. "A fat little Echidna for hungry old me!" He hissed and slithered towards his meal.

Python darted at Echidna faster than a tongue can flick. But Echidna managed to jump onto a huge log that lay almost right across the billabong.

And with Python, Native Cat, and Dingo close behind, Echidna ran across the log towards the other side.

He was only half-way across when suddenly the log gave a mighty shake.

"Wraaaaa!" roared Crocodile in a voice that made the whole billabong quake. "Who dares to run across my back!"

Whooosh! went his great tail, tossing tiny Echidna high into the air.

Down tumbled Echidna, right onto Crocodile's head. Snap! went Crocodile's cruel jaws. But too late!

With a terrified shriek Echidna scrambled to the billabong bank and dashed away, with Crocodile, Python, Native Cat, and Dingo close behind.

Just ahead loomed the tallest mountain Echidna had ever seen. "The Great One might be there," he thought. "That's the only place left. Oh, please, please let him be there!"

Close behind him Echidna could feel the hot, hungry, breath of his enemies. The thought of being their lunch spurred him on, and he reached the mountain just ahead of them.

Up the steep side he scurried, scrambling higher and higher. The mountain was so steep that soon the others were too scared to climb any further.

But further and further Echidna climbed. Up and up until the others became just tiny dots far below.

Just as he was feeling safe, Echidna felt a sudden rush of wind. Something sharp tore at his skin and hurt him. It was Eagle—clawing and squawking and hungry for food!

"Ah! Just in time for lunch!" Eagle screeched as she flapped at Echidna. "I haven't eaten all day!"

But Eagle's lunch was so frightened, it jumped away and scurried off.

Echidna hugged close to every little crevice and crack, trying to shelter from Eagle's sharp beak and clutching claws. Up and up he struggled, climbing higher. At last the clouds swirled around him, and hungry Eagle was lost to sight.

As Echidna neared the top of the mountain, a cold, thick mist swept in, covering everything with greyness. Soon the mist had made the day grow so gloomy, Echidna had to feel his way upwards. He could hardly see in front of him.

At last he reached up with a tiny paw. He felt about for something to hold, but nothing was there.

"Nothing?" he thought. His heart skipped a beat. Surely this was the top of the mountain. Carefully he pulled himself up and over the edge. He stood on the mountain top in the ghostly mist.

"Is . . . is anyone here?" he whispered, hardly daring to speak. But no answer came. "There's no one here," he thought. "My searching was all in vain."

But as he stood there, sad and alone, the breeze came gently blowing. Just for a moment the mist parted, and there . . . Echidna gasped! There, through the mist, was the Great One.

"Why have you come to my mountain?" a great voice boomed.

"Please . . . I have come for something to keep me safe," said Echidna, hardly daring to look.

"There is nothing left to give!" echoed the voice through the mist.

"But anything will do," pleaded Echidna. "Some leftover wings or teeth or . . . "

"There is nothing," said the great voice. "Nothing but a few old bones!"

"But please," cried Echidna. "You must give me something . . . "

"**Must?**" roared the voice angrily. "Must?" Then the Great One picked up the old bones that lay scattered around. Suddenly there was a crash of thunder. The whole mountain trembled and shook!

By the time the fearsome noise had faded and the mountain had become still once again, the Great One had vanished.

But the bones! Oh how Echidna wished he had never come to the mountain! All the bones the Great One had thrown were stuck in his skin. And try as he would, Echidna could not pull them out. The bones had become part of him.

"So," laughed Dingo when poor, sorry Echidna made his way to the bottom of the mountain. "What bony old teeth the Great One has given you."

"What bony old legs," laughed Native Cat.

"What bony old wings," mocked Eagle.

And as all his hungry enemies rushed in, little Echidna rolled himself up into a tiny ball and squeezed his eyes shut with fright. But something very strange happened as he waited for the end.

Dingo was the first to take a bite. As his teeth snapped shut on the bones, he gave a painful cry.

Next, Native Cat pounced on Echidna. She screamed as the bones stuck into her paws.

Crocodile took a bite and raced off howling horribly, with bones trailing from his jaws.

Python tried to wrap his coils around the bony little ball and slithered away hissing with pain.

Eagle squawked loudly as she landed on Echidna and flew off screeching, never to be seen again.

When at last everything was quiet, the spiky little ball slowly opened its eyes and looked about in surprise.

It was amazing. Echidna could hardly believe his eyes. His enemies had run away in fear of his old bones.

"Bones?" thought Echidna. "They're not just old bones. They're ... they're quills!" he laughed. "That's what they are. Nice, sharp quills. Oh, thank you, Great One. Thank you!"

And giving his nice new quills a proud little shake, Echidna waddled off into the bush, never to be bothered by the other animals ever again.

HOW EMU
Lost his Wings

There was a time, long ago, when Emu had the most wonderful wings in all the world.

They were so wide and so strong, he could fly faster than the wind and further than the sun.

Emu was proud of his great wings, and proud of his clever wife. For every year she hatched ten lovely chicks. All the chicks grew into big, strong Emus.

For as long as the other birds could remember, Emu had been their leader. The others were happy at this. For who else had such splendid wings? Or such fine, young chicks?

There was one bird, however, who was jealous of Emu—and this was Bustard.

Bustard also had large wings, though not quite as large as Emu's.

His wife also hatched ten chicks each year. But they never grew as big or as strong as Emu's chicks.

"Why should Emu be the leader of the bird tribe?" Bustard complained to his wife one day.

"Bustards are much more clever," said his wife.

"And much more handsome," Bustard added as he preened his feathers.

"You should teach Emu a lesson," said his wife.

"I will," agreed Bustard. "Then maybe I'll become the leader of the bird tribe."

Early next morning, long before the other birds were awake, Bustard flew off to the plains.

He hurried to Emu's favourite feeding place and settled down in the grass to wait.

When at last he spied Emu flying towards him, Bustard held his wings close to his sides. He tucked his feathers in so it looked like his wings were missing.

Emu landed nearby and began to eat the grass.

''Oh, Emu,'' Bustard called out slyly. ''Why do you fly through the air like that?''

"Fly?" asked Emu. "How else should a bird go?"

"Any common bird can fly," laughed the crafty Bustard. "But only a strong bird, a noble bird, can walk around on his legs."

Just then Emu noticed that Bustard's wings seemed to be missing.

"What has happened to your wings?" he asked.

"My wife and I have cut them off," Bustard replied. "Now we walk every-where instead."

Carefully keeping his wings tucked into his sides, Bustard walked around on his legs.

"See?" he said. "See what a fine walk I have?"

Emu watched with interest as Bustard strutted about.

"Your legs are even longer and stronger than mine," said Bustard slyly. "You could walk, too."

"Let me try it," said Emu. And he walked around to see how it felt.

"What a grand walk. What a noble walk," said Bustard as he watched Emu. "Imagine common old Magpie or Crow trying to walk like that. With their short legs they would look silly. That's why common birds have to fly everywhere!"

"Perhaps you are right," Emu replied. "I must go home to think about this."

He spread his wings to fly away but suddenly changed his mind. Instead, he tucked his wings into his sides and walked away, his head held high.

"Won't we look strange without our wings?" his wife worried.

"We will look grand," Emu replied as he picked up a sharp stone chopper. "You'll soon get used to it."

Next morning Bustard saw Emu walking across the plain towards him. He tucked his wings close to his sides and pretended he was busy eating the grass.

"Oh, Bustard," called Emu as he drew near. "You were right. My wife and I chopped our wings off last night. From now on we shall walk everywhere."

Emu walked around proudly to show Bustard.

"My wings hardly hurt at all now," said Emu happily. "And my legs are growing stronger all the time. Come on. I'll race you to that bush!"

Emu raced off as fast as he could. Bustard, however, spread his wings and flew to the tree.

How surprised Emu was to see Bustard land in the tree ahead of him.

"You said you had chopped your wings off!" cried Emu.

"You simple creature. I tricked you!" sneered Bustard. "Now I shall fly home to tell my wife that the leader of the birds has lost his precious wings!"

With an angry squawk Emu sprang at Bustard. But Bustard easily escaped him and flew away laughing with glee.

Bustard was sure that Emu would try to punish him. For many days he kept a careful watch. But Emu left him alone.

He was busy learning to use his legs. He found that the more he walked, the stronger they became.

Soon he was able to race across the plain in a streak of dust. Indeed, so swiftly could he run, the other birds could hardly keep up with him.

The seasons came and went. Spring was followed by summer. The bush became filled with the sounds of new-born birds.

They cackled and squabbled and screeched. They cried all the time for food. They kept their poor parents busy from morning to night.

Bustard and his wife had ten new chicks as usual. How proud they were of their hungry young brood.

One day they were out on the plain, catching grasshoppers and frogs and spiders and other delicious things that baby Bustards love to eat.

"Look," said Bustard with surprise. "Here comes Emu. And he only has two chicks with him!"

"Good morning," said Emu as he came upon them. "You both look worn out."

"That's because we have to work all day feeding our chicks," grumbled Bustard.

"It's not easy to look after ten hungry young ones," complained his wife.

"Yes. That's the problem if you have too many chicks," agreed Emu. "You can never find enough food for them. So they don't grow very big. What a pity."

"Where are all your chicks?" asked Bustard. "I can only see two of them."

"That's because my wife and I kept the biggest two and killed the rest," said Emu.

"Killed them?" gasped the astonished Bustards.

"That's right," said Emu happily. "Now we can give these two all the food they need. They're growing so fast; too. See how much bigger than your children they are? Soon they'll be strong, healthy Emus."

The bustards could hardly believe their ears. They walked around the two Emu chicks and looked at them closely.

"They are indeed big, strong chicks," whispered Bustard's wife. "Much bigger than our own."

"Perhaps it is better to raise only two children," agreed her husband. "Come, wife. We must think about this." And he led his brood away.

"Just look at our greedy chicks," Bustard's wife twittered angrily when they arrived home. "We work from morning to night to feed them. Yet they still cry for more!"

"Emu is right," said Bustard, nodding his head. "Let's keep the biggest two and kill the rest."

"Yes," agreed his wife. "And we will feed the ones we kill to the ones we keep. Then they will grow even bigger than Emu's children!"

So late that night, when their chicks were fast asleep, the Bustards killed eight of them.

Emu was not really surprised at what he saw the very next morning.

The Bustards were coming across the plain—and only two chicks were with them.

"We have taken your advice," Bustard said as he came upon Emu. "We have killed all our children except these two. Don't you agree they'll be fine, strong birds?"

To the Bustard's surprise, Emu began to laugh.

"You stupid creatures," he chuckled. "Do you really think I would kill my beautiful chicks? Just you watch."

Emu called to his wife who had been hiding behind a bush. She hurried over, and behind her came their ten handsome Emu chicks.

"You see?" laughed Emu. "We did not kill our chicks at all. I fooled you! A bird's true strength does not come from his wings. It comes from the number of children he has. And you have killed most of your children, you cruel and foolish birds!"

Without another word Emu gathered up his family and led them across the plain. And behind him the Bustards wept to think how foolish they had been.

All this happened a long, long time ago. But even today Emus still have no wings.

Not that they really care. For their legs have grown big and strong. And Emus can run as fast as the wind and as far as the sun.

And the foolish Bustards? Try as they will, they can only manage to hatch two children.

That is the punishment they received for trying to fool the great leader of the bird tribe.

How
WATER-RAT
Found Fire

There was a time long ago when the animals had no fire to keep themselves warm. When winter came and the cold wind blew, the poor creatures shivered and shook all night.

But the coldest of all was Water-Rat. He and his family lived in a burrow beside a large pond. Each day he had to swim through the pond in search of food, and in winter the water was as cold as ice.

A long tunnel led from the bank of the pond to Water-Rat's burrow. Whenever he came home, he would walk along the tunnel, soaked to the skin, with water dripping everywhere.

"Don't come in. Stay in the tunnel!" his wife would shout. "You're splashing water all over us. We're cold enough already!"

So Water-Rat had to wait in the tunnel until he was dry. But even inside the burrow he couldn't get warm. The wind blew in from the pond. It whistled through the tunnel and rushed around, making Water-Rat and his family miserable and cold.

"Now that our children are growing bigger, this burrow is too small," said Water-Rat's wife one day. "You must dig a new burrow, one that is further away from the pond, so the wind doesn't blow in."

"I'm too busy hunting for food," said Water-Rat. "Who will feed the children if I have to spend my time digging a new burrow?"

But his wife kept nagging and complaining until at last Water-Rat agreed to dig a new burrow.

He began by digging a long tunnel. At first the work was easy, for the earth was soft and Water-Rat's teeth were sharp and his claws were strong. But the further he got from the pond, the harder the earth became. To make matters worse, large rocks and tree roots began to appear. ·

One day, as he was gnawing at a large root, his teeth slipped and struck against a rock. This caused a sudden bright flash of light that gave Water-Rat quite a shock. He backed out of the tunnel and hurried to tell his wife.

"When I bit into the rock there was a strange flash of light!" he told her.

"Nonsense," scoffed his wife. "You just imagined it!"

Water-Rat returned to his digging. A little later his teeth struck another rock. There was another flash of light and a small spark flew through the air and landed on his paw.

"Yiii! That's hot!" squeaked Water-Rat as his fur sizzled.

He hurried from the tunnel and sat in his burrow to think about what had happened.

"How odd," he thought. "Each time my teeth strike against a rock, they cause a flash of light. And it's hot! How very strange."

Water-Rat did no more digging that day. Instead, he sat and thought about the tiny sparks he had seen. Late that night as he and his family lay snuggled against each other, trying to keep warm, he had the strangest dream.

He dreamed that their burrow was no longer cold and damp. It was warm and dry, and the warmth came from some dancing sparks. They were not small sparks, like those that had flashed so briefly in the tunnel. They were large and bright and they never went out.

Next morning when Water-Rat woke up, he hurried into the tunnel without even having breakfast. Once he was inside, he chose the biggest rock he could find and bit into it. Once again, a tiny spark flashed brightly.

Water-Rat picked up two smaller rocks and struck them together. Another spark flew out.

"How can I make these bright little spirits stay?" Water-Rat wondered. "They disappear so quickly."

Now it happened that a small pile of leaves lay nearby. As Water-Rat struck the rocks together for the second time, a spark jumped onto a leaf. The leaf glowed briefly and a tiny wisp of smoke curled into the air.

This excited Water-Rat. He made more sparks jump onto the leaves. Suddenly, when one of the leaves glowed faintly, he bent down to peer at it. This time it didn't go out.

"The spark has stayed on the leaf!" he squeaked.

As he spoke, his breath made the leaf glow more brightly Water-Rat saw this and blew on it gently. The leaf burst into flames, which quickly spread to other leaves. Soon a big blaze burned merrily in the tunnel.

Water-Rat called his new discovery "fire". And he spent most of that morning learning about it. He learned how to feed it leaves and twigs and to make it grow. He even learned how to carry a small fire around on the end of a stick and start it growing again in a fresh pile of leaves.

When at last he proudly carried the fire into the burrow, his family could hardly believe their eyes.

"Take it away!" his wife shrieked in fright.

"Help! It will bite us!" his children squeaked as they backed away.

Water-Rat just laughed and set the fire down in a corner. As the family felt their home growing warmer, they realised that Water-Rat had discovered a wonderful thing.

Soon they were sitting close to the fire, enjoying its cosy warmth. For the first time in all their winters their burrow was snug and dry.

All through winter the Water-Rats enjoyed the glowing warmth of the fire. It wasn't long before Water-Rat learned how to cook food over the flames. Their meals tasted much better after that. They had never known food could be so delicious.

But when spring arrived, Water-Rat's wife began to complain.

"The fire is filling our home with smoke," she told her husband. "It hurts my eyes. Why can't you take it outside?"

Water-Rat was quite happy to leave the fire where it was, but his wife kept complaining until finally he set the fire on the bank beside their home.

That night as Water-Rat sat beside his fire, he saw the eyes of other animals watching from the darkness. The others had never seen such a glorious thing before and never had they felt such marvellous warmth. They slowly crept closer and soon Water-Rat heard them calling out.

"Water-Rat," the animals called. "The shining spirits feel so warm. Can we sit beside them?"

Now Water-Rat was really a selfish creature. He did not mind sharing his fire with his family, but he would never dream of sharing it with the other animals.

"I found the fire!" he called out to the eyes shining in the darkness. "It's mine alone. I won't share it!"

So the cold and wretched animals shivered in the night while Water-Rat warmed himself beside the dancing flames.

The next night Water-Rat cooked his dinner over the fire. The breeze carried the delicious, exciting smells through the trees and soon a circle of eyes appeared.

"Water-Rat, we have never smelled food as good as that," the animals called. "Couldn't you share your fire with us?"

"No!" Water-Rat shouted angrily. "I won't share it with anyone!"

The disappointed animals gathered together in the darkness.

"How mean Water-Rat is," Koala muttered.

"Why should we freeze in winter, while he stays warm?" growled Kangaroo.

"And why should he be the only one to have such delicious food?" Tortoise grumbled. "I'll sneak up and take some of his fire."

"Yes! If he won't share his fire, we'll take it!" the others cried.

So Tortoise crept quietly through the grass. But as he drew closer, the bright light from the fire revealed him to Water-Rat.

Water-Rat had been expecting just this. As soon as he saw Tortoise he quickly splashed water onto the flames and the fire went out.

"There!" Water-Rat laughed. "Now you can have as much fire as you want!"

And he hurried inside his burrow to finish his meal.

The next night, as Water-Rat sat beside his fire, the unhappy animals watched and wondered how they could take some for themselves.

"Maybe I can do it," said Kangaroo. "After all, I'm much faster than Tortoise."

So Kangaroo hopped swiftly towards the fire. But Water-Rat heard him bouncing along and quickly splashed water onto the flames.

"You'll have to be faster than that!" he laughed.

The following night the animals tried again. This time Kookaburra decided he should do it.

"After all," he said. "I don't bounce noisily like Kangaroo."

So Kookaburra flew straight towards the fire. But Water-Rat heard the flapping of his wings and quickly put the flames out.

"Ha!" he laughed meanly. "You'll have to be quieter than that!"

A little later the sorry animals gathered once more in the darkness.

"We'll never get any fire," moaned Wombat. "We might as well give up."

"We may not be able to get any fire," said Kangaroo. "But I know someone who can!"

"Who?" the others asked hopefully.

"Eagle," Kangaroo replied.

"Yes, Eagle!" the others agreed excitedly. "Maybe he can help us."

So early next morning the animals went to Eagle and told him their tale. Eagle listened to them thoughtfully, then spoke.

"I have seen Water-Rat's fire from high in the sky," he said. "It is something that all creatures should have. Before this day is over, I will make Water-Rat share it with you."

Before the animals could thank him, Eagle had gone. With a few beats of his powerful wings he rose into the air and was soon lost to sight above the clouds.

Later that morning, Water-Rat peeped out from his burrow. He glanced all around as usual to see if anyone was about, then he swam across the pond.

He didn't notice the tiny speck floating far above him in the sky.

Eagle, however, had been waiting for just that moment. As soon as Water-Rat began swimming across the pond, Eagle dived through the air almost faster than the eye could follow.

Water-Rat was barely halfway across the water when a brown streak dropped from the sky. He shrieked in fright as he felt Eagle's claws wrap tightly around him!

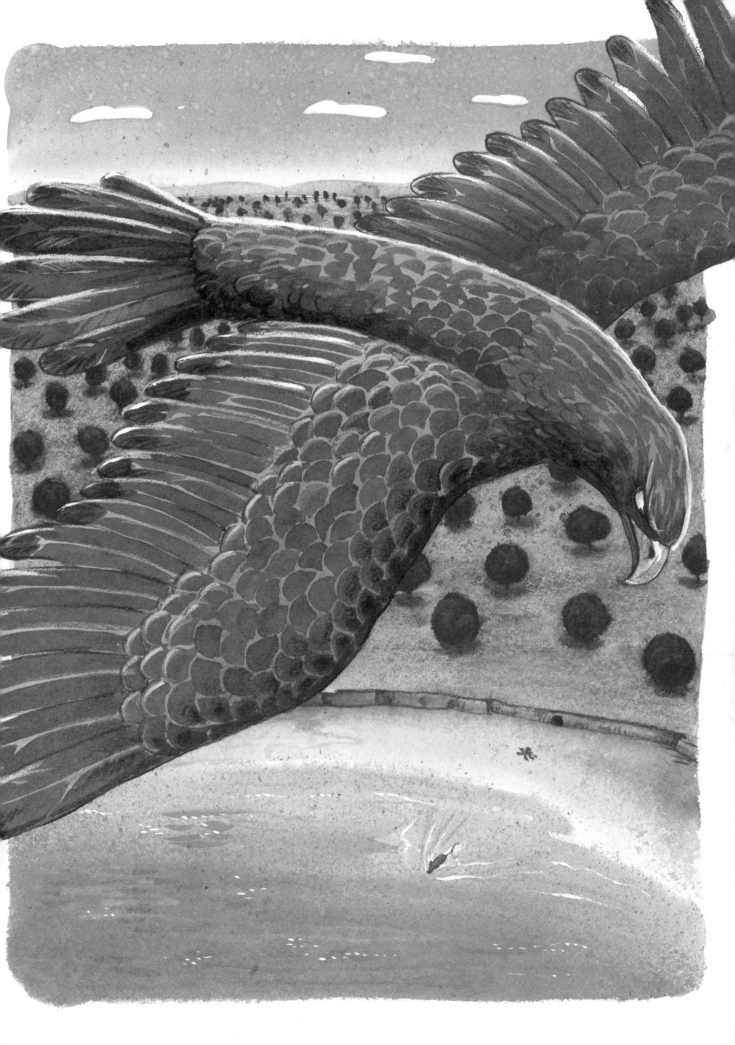

Water-Rat was terrified. He saw the world rushing away beneath him until his familiar pond was just a tiny blue dot far below. He thought that soon he would be a tasty lunch for Eagle's hungry chicks.

"Oh, please don't feed me to your children!" Water-Rat pleaded. "I'll do anything, I promise, anything, if you let me return to my pond."

"If I let you go now, you'll return to your pond faster than you'd like to," chuckled Eagle.

Water-Rat looked down at the world far below. He shook with fear as he imagined himself falling through the air like a stone.

"There is nothing you can do for me," Eagle continued, "but there is something you can do for the other creatures."

"Oh, tell me! Please tell me. I'll do anything!" squealed Water-Rat.

"You can share with them the fire you have discovered," said Eagle.

"What?" squeaked Water-Rat, in a sudden rage. "Share my precious fire? Never!"

Straight away, he felt Eagle's claws starting to loosen.

"Wait!" shrieked Water-Rat fearfully. "I'll do it, I promise. I'll share my fire with them!"

"Very well," said Eagle. "I'll return you to your pond. But if you don't keep your promise, I'll come back for you. And you'll have one last journey into the sky!"

So Eagle returned Water-Rat to his pond. The fear of taking that last journey into the sky helped Water-Rat keep his promise. He shared his fire and the animals were happy.

Of course, all this happened a long time ago. But even today Water-Rat is not a popular creature. He does not mix with other animals and he has very few friends.

For every winter, when the animals gather by their fires to keep warm, they remember Water-Rat—and how mean he was to them so long ago.